For my brother Michael, the original Roger
and for Amber, extraordinary cat — M.K.
For Froggie — A.A.

VIKING
Published by the Penguin Group
Viking Penguin, a division of Penguin Books USA Inc.,
375 Hudson Street, New York, New York 10014, U.S.A.
Penguin Books Australia Ltd, Ringwood, Victoria, Australia
Penguin Books Canada Ltd, 10 Alcorn Avenue, Toronto, Ontario, Canada M4V 3B2
Penguin Books (N.Z.) Ltd, 182-190 Wairau Road, Auckland 10, New Zealand

First published in Great Britain in 1992 by ABC, **All** **B**ooks for **Ch**ildren,
a division of The All Children's Company Ltd.

First American edition published in 1992

1   3   5   7   9   10   8   6   4   2
Text copyright © Monica Kulling, 1992
Illustrations copyright © Alex Ayliffe, 1992
All rights reserved

Library of Congress Catalog Card Number: 91-50801
ISBN: 0-670-84480-2
Printed in Hong Kong

I Hate You,

Marmalade!

Story by Monica Kulling • *Illustrations by* Alex Ayliffe

Viking

Roger's mother brought home a cat. A fat, furry orange CAT. "Now, Roger, this is Marmalade. Be nice!"

Marmalade looked at Roger with one big yellow eye while she washed her face.

"This is my house now," she said with every lick.

At bedtime, there was a big surprise for Roger. In the middle of his bed lay Marmalade. She looked like a plump pumpkin. One eye opened. "Forget it, kid," Marmalade seemed to say. "I was here first."

Roger decided to sleep in his beanbag chair.
It wasn't very comfortable, but it was better
than moving Marmalade.

At breakfast, Roger had another surprise. Sitting in his favorite chair, without a care in the world, was Marmalade. Roger hissed, "Go away. Shoo!" Marmalade hissed back, "Get lossst!" Roger sat in his father's chair. Marmalade just sat and stared. Then she closed her eyes and yawned a great big fangy yawn.

Roger finished breakfast quickly and
went out to play with his new fire-
truck. But Marmalade was sitting
in the driver's seat, grinning
a fire-cat grin.

"Go away, you fat
cat," Roger said.

He picked up a stick and waved it at Marmalade. The orange cat arched her back and hissed. "Sssscat! You sssilly boy!" She scratched Roger on the hand.

Roger ran inside.
"Mom!" he hollered.
"Marmalade scratched me!"

Mother put a Band-Aid on Roger's scratch.
"Were you bothering Marmalade?" she asked.
"No. She bothers me," replied Roger.
"I hate Marmalade!"
"Now, Roger. Marmalade's not that bad.
Just be nice to her and she'll be nice to
you. It's easy."

When Roger went back outside, Marmalade
was gone. But Alison was standing by his fire-truck.
Alison was older than Roger and was always
picking on him.

"Go away," said Roger.

Alison ignored him. "Wow! Is that yours?"
she asked, beeping the truck's horn.

"Get away," said Roger. "Leave it alone."

Alison didn't want to leave the fire-truck alone.
She wanted a ride. She was too big to sit in it, so
she put one foot on the seat and scooted along
with her other foot on the ground.

"Beep, beep!" said Alison. "Here comes the
fire-truck to the rescue!"

"Give me back my truck!" yelled Roger, as he
ran after Alison. But she was too busy driving to
the rescue to stop. She was going so fast, Roger
was afraid she would break his truck.

Suddenly there was a terrific YOWL, then
a gigantic GROWL and an enormous HISSS!

Marmalade hurtled across the garden with her back arched and her tail fluffed out.

Alison didn't wait to discover
what Marmalade would do next. She
pulled her foot out of the truck, then ran
straight home.

Roger heard Alison's door slam. Then he went
into his own house. He came back out with a piece
of roast beef. "Here you are, Marmalade," he said.
"Thanks for saving my truck."

Marmalade looked at the meat. She looked at Roger and kept on looking at him while she ate.

At breakfast the next morning
Roger's favorite chair was empty.
Marmalade was sitting in Dad's chair.
Dad came in for breakfast, took one
look at Marmalade, and sat in Mom's chair.

After breakfast Roger went out to pedal his fire-truck. Marmalade was waiting on the hood. Roger climbed in and pedaled down the driveway. Marmalade stayed for the ride, grinning her fire-cat grin.

At dinner, Dad asked Roger, "How are you and
Marmalade getting along these days?"

Roger looked at the furry orange cat. Marmalade
winked her yellow eyes at him.

"She's OK, I guess," he replied.
He patted the fat cat on the head.
Marmalade raced her motor.
"Same to you, kid," she seemed
to be saying. "Same to you."